'Oh heeeeeeeeeeeeeeeeeeeeeeeeeeeeee eeeeeeeeeeeeeeeeeeeeeeeeeeeeeeeeeeeeeeeelp!' Eppie and Zeke yelled together as they wandered around the ghost ship's deck looking for help and bashing into ropes and masts until they accidentally walked off the gangplank where they were swallowed by a killer whale, spurted out of his blow hole and thrown back onto the ghost ship's deck.

**Also available by
Gretel Killeen in Red Fox**

My Sister's a Yo-yo

My Sister's an Alien

My Sister's a Sea Slug

My Sister's a Burp

My Sister's a Full Stop

my Sister's a Nightmare

MY SISTER'S A NIGHTMARE
A RED FOX BOOK 0 099 46409 8

Published in Great Britain by Red Fox,
an imprint of Random House Children's Books

PRINTING HISTORY
First published in Australia by Random House Australia Pty Ltd, 2000
Red Fox edition published, 2005

1 3 5 7 9 10 8 6 4 2

Copyright © Gretel Killeen, 2000
Illustrations copyright © Gretel Killeen, 2000

Papers used by Random House Children's Books are natural, recyclable products
made from wood grown in sustainable forests. The manufacturing processes conform
to the environmental regulations of the country of origin.

Set in 17/21pt Bembo Schoolbook

Red Fox books are published by Random House Children's Books,
61–63 Uxbridge Road, London W5 5SA,
a division of The Random House Group Ltd,
in Australia by Random House Australia (Pty) Ltd,
20 Alfred Street, Milsons Point, Sydney, NSW 2061, Australia,
in New Zealand by Random House New Zealand Ltd,
18 Poland Road, Glenfield, Auckland 10, New Zealand,
and in South Africa by Random House (Pty) Ltd,
Endulini, 5A Jubilee Road, Parktown 2193, South Africa

THE RANDOM HOUSE GROUP Limited Reg. No. 954009

A CIP catalogue record for this book is available from the British Library.

Printed and bound in Great Britain by Cox & Wyman Ltd, Reading, Berkshire

www.kidsatrandomhouse.co.uk

gretEl KiLLeen

my Sister's a Nightmare

Illustrated by
Zeke and Eppie

RED FOX

A message from your author ...

G'day and welcome to the sixth book in the *My Sister's* series. Don't worry if you haven't read all the other books so far because there's a pile of time to eat them up and know about Eppie and Zeke's intergalactic travel, underwater adventures and being stuck inside their mother's gizzards. But one thing you should know before you start this book is that Eppie and Zeke are Australian and that means they can use words that you might not understand. Like **Vegemite**, which is a yummy food spread that looks a bit like black snot. Or **grot**, which is someone who's really grubby. Or **bandicoot**, which is a furry animal that is about the size of a big sausage dog. Or **slippery-dip** which is a slide. Or **slater** which is a creepy grey insect with heaps of legs.

So **love** this book, have fun and don't eat any grotty bandicoots covered in vegemite with a slater on your head.

It's not every day that you find yourself stuck inside someone else's nightmare. But then it's not every day that your sister shrinks to the size of a strawberry, gets a yo-yo tangled in her hair and ends up in outer space where she has to be rescued by you! And it's not every day that you return from space riding on a meteor and the amazing speed stretches you and your sister very long and thin like pieces of spaghetti so that when you finally do get home you get sucked down

1

the bathroom plughole, zapped by an electric eel, snuggled by a shark (who's pretending to be seaweed), rescued by a merprincess, attacked by soldier crabs, disguised as sea slugs, stranded on a desert island, evaporated like water droplets, and delivered by the stork to your very own back garden where your mother promptly swallows you.

And then it's not every day that you have to travel all the way through your mother's veins and gizzards and heart and brain to save your mum's life, and then finally escape out her nose, in a powerful sneeze with huge blobs of snot, and end up squished right inside the book of fairytales she's reading.

Little Red Riding Hood

The little book of favourite childrens stories.

So it's not every day that you get burped on by a giant, or you crash into a pond on a witch's broom, or you get toasted by a fire-breathing dragon, or a pig tries to marry you, or Tarman tries to rescue you, or a wishing well tries to eat you, or the Golden Goose gives you a taxi ride to the EXIT sign but you accidentally go out the wrong door and end up

inside your mother's nightmare . . .

but that's what had happened so far today.

'Help!' yelled tiny Eppie in the spooky kooky darkness as she sat like a toadstool on the deck of the ghost pirate ship.

'Heeeeeeeeeeeeeeeeeeee

eeeeeeeeeeeeeeeeeeeeeeeeee
eeeeeeeeeeeeeeeeeeeeeeeeee
eeeeeeeeeeeeeeeeeeeeeeeeee
eeeeeeeeeeeeeeeeeeeeeeeeee
eeeeelp!'

'Oh be quiet,' said tiny Zeke.

'Oh be quiet yourself,' said Eppie,
'because when I sit here yelling
heeeeeeeeeeeeeeeeeeeeeeeeeeeeeeeeeeee
eeeeeeeeelp I am not yelling it at you!'

'Oh really,' said Zeke in a smarty-pants
voice that sounded like he had a prune
up his nose. 'Well who are you yelling to
then? The thousand and one spit-covered
rats who are waiting to nibble your toes?
The ghoul in the ship's kitchen who's
waiting to boil you? Or the four-legged
toilet brush who's flying near your head
and looks a lot like my teacher Miss
Snailheadface?'

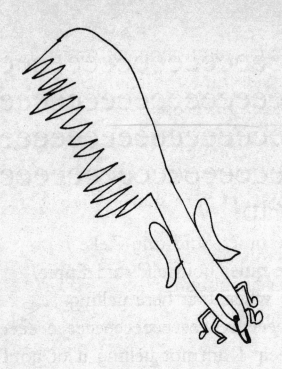

'For your information, bad-breath brother,' said Eppie as she sat in the thick-as-goop darkness, 'I was yelling it to anyone who's nice and caring and happens to be in the area.'

Well Zeke just laughed and laughed at his sister (because that's what brothers do) and then he burped in her ear and said very loudly:

'Well aren't you about as smart as a pig's bum because the chances of finding anyone nice on a ghost ship are absolutely **nought-er-ooony!**'

Then all of a sudden a blind bat picked Zeke up in his very sharp pointy claws and spun him in a circle in the air . . .

'Well even though it is a nightmare I'm sure we'll meet someone nice,' Eppie said, as she ignored Zeke hovering over her head and crawled in the dark along the deck until she slid for thirty seconds on a massive blob of seagull poo. 'I mean it is our mother's nightmare after all, and I reckon the worst nightmare that she ever has is that she can't get the stains out of our school uniforms.'

Suddenly Zeke was dropped from the sky and landed head first in a Halloween pumpkin.

'Oh stop mucking around Zeke,' growled Eppie, 'and help me find an escape hatch that will get us safely home.' Then tiny Eppie moved a little to the right and fell

whooooooooo ooooooooooo ooooooooooah

through the gap between two deck planks

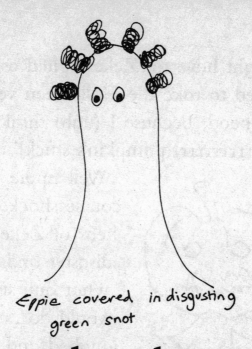

Eppie covered in disgusting green snot

and landed **splat phwat** splosh in a very big bottle of her third worst nightmare . . . disgusting green blubby snot.

'Ho ho giggle giggle he he ha,' Zeke laughed as Eppie slowly climbed up the ladder and landed exhausted back on the deck. 'You look like a green ghost.'

'And you look the most handsome you've ever been,' said Eppie. 'You should wear that pumpkin more often.'

'I might have to,' Zeke replied as he struggled to take the Halloween vegetable off his head, 'because I (ugh) think (agh) the (arrrrrrrrr) pumpkin's stuck!'

Well Eppie was of course shocked to hear of Zeke's disaster and did what any sister would do . . . she laughed and laughed and laughed. 'A ha ha ha ha he he ho hugh hugh hugh hehehehehhehe hhehehe tittle tittle guffaw guffaw a ha ha ha ha ha h ah ah ah ah ha ha haha ha ha ha ha ha ahha ha ha ha ha ha ha ha ha ha ha ha ha ha ha ha ha ahhhhhhhhhhh.' In fact Eppie laughed for such a long time that as she was clutching her stomach with glee the snot

she was wearing all over her head and
body began to set rock hard.

'Oh h-e---e-e-e-LP!'

screamed Eppie.

'I can't help you,' said Zeke from inside
the pumpkin, 'until you help me.'

'Well I can't help you,' Eppie replied,
'until you help me.'

'Oh heeeeeeeeeeeeeeeeeeeeeeeeeeeeeee
eeeeeeeeeeeeeeeeeeeeeeeeeeeeeeeelp!'
Eppie and Zeke yelled together as they
wandered around the ghost ship's deck
looking for help and bashing into ropes
and masts until they accidentally walked
off the gangplank where they were
swallowed by a killer whale, spurted out
of his blow hole and thrown back onto
the ghost ship's deck.

'Oh **heeeeeeeeeeeeeeeeeeeeeeeeeeeeee
eeeeeeeeeeeeeeeeeeeeeeeeeeeeeeeelp!**'
yelled Eppie and Zeke together.

11

'I'll help yoooooooooooooooooooooo oooooooooooooooooooooo,' said a voice that sounded a little like Fart Simpson.

'Where are you?' said Zeke.

'I'm standing next to you,' said the voice, 'but you won't see me because I'm invisible.'

'Oh fabulous,' said Zeke, 'so now we can't tell if you're a pimple-covered dragon or a poop smothered jellyblubber and we won't have a clue at all if you're our dream come true or just another nightmare.'

'Well, for your information,' said the voice, 'all the girls used to say I'm a dream come true.'

('Yeah, that's what the boys say about me,' said Eppie.

'Oh shrivel up like a worm's butt,' said Zeke.)

'In fact,' said the voice, 'I used to be a perfect playful piddling puppy called Pat until Dr Freckle and Miss Hide 'n' Seek made me quite invisible.'

←he's here

↑
Invisible Pat The Pup

Well Eppie and Zeke weren't convinced until Pat the Pup piddled on Eppie's leg and Eppie and Zeke decided to trust him. But now the problem was that Pat only had paws and, no matter how hard he tried, Pat could not remove Zeke's pumpkin head. So Pat howled and barked for his right-hand man. And suddenly a right hand appeared.

'Hello,' said the hand. 'My name is Right, and don't ever get that wrong. Now I'm here to help you out because that's what we do in this nightmare.'

13

Smugly Eppie thumped Zeke in an 'I told you there'd be someone nice here' way, but she thumped him so hard with her crusty snot-covered arm that he rolled all the way up the deck like a baseball and then rolled all the way back down again.

'Anyway, as I was saying,' said Right as he ordered Pat the Pup to lick the snot off Eppie's face while he gently tried to remove Zeke's pumpkin head, 'we all help each other. Ugh,' he grunted. 'Agh,' he heaved. 'Oooogh,' he pulled. 'We help each other while we fight the evil Dr Freckle and Miss Hide 'n' Seek.'

And then the pumpkin came off Zeke's head and Right took one little look at Zeke and loudly screeched,

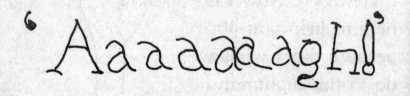

'Aaaaaaagh!'

'I told you that you looked better with that pumpkin on,' mumbled Eppie.

'Quick, run for your life Pat the Pup!' bellowed the Right hand as he let his fingers do the running and scampered out of sight. And with that, invisible Pat also disappeared . . . or Zeke and Eppie assumed he disappeared. (But in all honesty it was hard to tell because Pat the Pup was **invisible** so he could have stayed in exactly the same place right then and there, or stood on his head, or tied himself in a knot, or given some revolting long googly-tongue-kiss to his invisible girlfriend, Kit the Kat! So I guess it would be more accurate to say that invisible Pat the Pup may or may not have gone away.)

'Oh boohoo boohoo boohoo,' Eppie boohooed.

'Oh b–b–b–be quiet,' said Zeke, 'or I won't bother to tell you that a vampire is coming up behind you and he wants to suck your b-blooooooood.'

'Oh, nice try, Zeke,' said Eppie. 'I don't see any vampire.'

'That's because it's behind you!' squeaked Zeke.

And so Eppie turned round to look behind her, but she still didn't see a vampire.

'It's behind you, I said!' squawked Zeke.

So Eppie turned round again and again but still she didn't see a vampire.

'It's behind you!!!!!!!!!!!!!!!!!!!!' roared Zeke once more.

So Eppie turned round again and again and again and again but still she DID NOT SEE A VAMPIRE!

'It is behind you!' bellowed Zeke.

So finally, completely annoyed, before she poked Zeke to death with her rude finger,

Eppie turned round very quickly, one more time . . .

and then promptly got so dizzy she collapsed
backwards

and fell onto the ghost pirate ship deck.

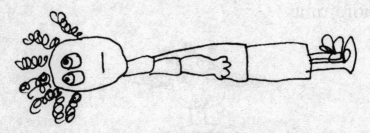

'Outh,' said the sort of voice that
someone with fangs would have. 'Outh.
Geth off me, wouldth you!'

'Who are you?' said Eppie.

'I'm the vampire whoooth come to
thuck your blurd.'

'E-p-p-p-peeeeeeeee!' stuttered Z-Z-Z-

Zeke. 'It's a-a-a v-v-v-vampire and it wants to sssssssssuck your bblood!!!!!!'

'Heeeeeeeeeeeeeeeeeeeeeeeeeelp!' screamed Eppie.

'Heeeeeeeeeeeeeeeeeeeeeeeeeelp!' screamed Zeke.

'Oh for heventh thake be quieth everyone, you're badly affecting my appetithe,' said the vampire. 'And by the way, would thomeone turn the lightth on pleathe tho I can get a better look at my dinner.'

Well someone did turn the lights on – presumably invisible Pat the Pup, but possibly his girlfriend Kit the Kat or their pet person called Peter.

↑
The Invisible
Pat The Pup

↑
The Invisible
Kit The Kat

↑
The Invisible Pet,
Pete The Person

'Oh my ghoulishness!' gasped the vampire as he took a look at Eppie.

19

'Get me out of here!'

Then the vampire ran as fast as anyone can wearing shiny black shoes and a very long cape and he tripped over his fangs not once, not twice, but forty-three times, making his fangs quite blunt in the process! And as the vampire hurled himself over the side of the ship and into the deep dark scary sea, his last words were heard to echo through the eerie light,

'I'm
becoming
a
vegetarian!'

• • • • • • • • • •

Eppie was devastated that the vampire had screamed at her. 'Why did the vampire scream when he saw me?' she said, 'I think I look absolutely gorgeous.'

'Are you joking?' roared Zeke, as he doubled up with laughter. 'You're about as gorgeous as a lizard's gizzards!'

lizard's gizzards

'Well why didn't he scream at you, Zeke?' continued Eppie. 'I feel like screaming at your frog-like face every single frightening time I see or hear or smell you!'

'Well maybe the vampire was screaming at me,' replied Zeke. 'Maybe he took one look at my magnificent muscles and thought hooly-ma-looly it's Arnold Schwarzenneger.'

'More like Arnold Schwarzenneger's pet ferret,' mumbled Eppie as she sat down once more on the cold wet deck of the ghost pirate ship.

'What did you say?' said Zeke.

'Nothing,' said Eppie.

'What did you say?' said Zeke.

'Nothing,' repeated Eppie.

'Nothing what?' said Zeke.

'Nothing nothing,' said Eppie.

'Nothing nothing what?' said Zeke.

'Nothing nothing nothing,' said Eppie.

'Nothing nothing nothing what?' said Zeke.

'Nothing nothing nothing noth—' started Eppie but before she could finish she was rudely interrupted by a three-bottomed pirate flying through the air, heading like a missile straight for Zeke and Eppie, and yelling at the very top of his voice,

22

'I am a kamikaze pirate!'

'What did he say?' Eppie asked Zeke as the pirate came rocketing towards them.

'I think he said he's a kamikaze plate,' said Zeke, 'and I think that is a type of fried rice which has extra chicken in it.'

extra chicken

chicken

fried rice

'No, I am not a plate of fried rice,' said the pirate, 'I am a kamikaze PIRATE. And that is a pirate who is willing to sacrifice his life in order to rid the world of a wicked menace.'

Well Eppie and Zeke had no idea what this pirate was on about. Not only had he torpedoed towards them three times already during their conversation and completely missed each time, but he also seemed to have confused Zeke and Eppie with some sort of terrible world-threatening evil, like global warming or gas warfare or those shiny tight black shorts that cyclists like to wear.

dreadful black shorts

'I'm sorry,' said Eppie, very politely to the pilot, um plate, um pirate. 'But I think you've mistaken us for somebody else.'

'Oh no I haven't, me hearties,' laughed the pirate. 'A ha ha ha ha ha. Because if there are two creatures in Nightmare Land that we would never confuse with anyone else, they are you two . . . you suspicious specimens, you weedy, wicked weirdos, you frightening fools, you vicked villains, you hideously horrible horrendous human beings . . . You two, standing right here before me . . . otherwise known as . . .
Dr Freckle and
Miss Hide 'n' Seek!'

'Oh yes,' continued the kamikaze pirate, 'I know that I'm right because I am the chief detective at the Nightmare World Pirate Department where we're thinking of starting our own TV show called "NWPD Oooooooo's". See, we received word that you two creeps were wandering around here all alone without your poisonous potions, and we decided that this would be an excellent time to capture you and feed you both to the kid-eating underwater spider, called Saliva!'

And then the pirate sang a song as he danced a jig, and wiggled his bottoms and a thousand ghosts swayed in the background singing back-up vocals and wearing miniskirts over their sheets.

'We don't care how SCARY *you are, you're a curse to this land and have gone too far so we'll feed you to the underwater Saliva, 'cause she's a spider . . . and soon we'll find ya wriggling and jiggling and tickling inside her! A ha a ha aha ha ha ha!'*

And with that a giant purple flying rat scooped up Eppie and Zeke in his big rat wings so he could fly them over the menacing black water and drop them in the sea for the spider's breakfast.

'Ahem,' said Eppie in a squishy sort of voice because she was being squeezed too

tightly by the wings. 'Um, excuse me, flying rat, but I was just wondering why they sang that we're um, ah, scary?'

'Is it because Eppie is so ugly?' said Zeke.

'Well,' said the rat as he sort of clumsily wriggle–hopped over to the side of the ship while he tried to keep Eppie and Zeke wrapped tightly in his wings. 'Obviously we said that you're scary because you two are Dr Freckle and Miss Hide 'n' Seek and with the use of your scientific potions you can turn everything in Nightmare World into anything that you want.'

'I beg your pardon?' said Zeke.

'Oh please don't pick on me,' said the rat, and his eyes started to fill with tears as he leapt off the side of the ghost ship with Zeke and Eppie wrapped up in his wings. 'Please just let me drop you into the big black sea and watch you get eaten by the giant spider.' And with that the flying rat went to wipe away his tears with his wings and Zeke and Eppie fell right out of his clutches.

Down

and

down

and

down they tumbled, down down down down, into the deep dark sea.

SPLASH!!

SPLASH!!

SPLASH!!

But the weird thing was that the sea didn't feel like water . . . because it was sort of soft . . . and warm . . . and sort of sloppy instead.

'Why is this sea so soft and warm and sloppy?' asked Eppie in surprise as she floated luxuriously on her back.

'And how come it's bright red?' said Zeke in between his duck dives and tumbles and underwater backflips.

29

'Well, maybe we're not in the deep dark sea,' said Eppie.

'You're not,' said a big bubbling voice. 'I think you're inside me.'

Eppie and Zeke tried looking around to see where the voice had come from, but even though they looked up and down and round about they could not see a thing.

'I think we're inside your mushy brain,' said Eppie.

'Well, at least I have a brain,' said Zeke.

'Not a very good one,' interrupted that strange bubbly voice once again.

'What do you mean I don't have a good brain?' said Zeke.

'I mean,' blurted the bubbling voice, 'that you can't have a good brain because if you did then you would realise that you're not inside anyone's brain at all and are in fact just bobbing around inside me! And I'm a huge saucepan of blood porridge.'

'A saucepan of what?' said Zeke.

'Aaaaaaaaaaaaaaaaaaa aaaaaagggggggggggggg hhhhhhhhhhhhhhhhhhh hhhhhhhhhhhhhhhhhhh hhhhhhh!'

'Oh calm down,' said Eppie. 'You heard what he said . . . and I really don't know what you're so disgusted about. I mean, it can't be any worse than Mum's cooking.'

'But we didn't swim in Mum's cooking, Eppie! We just ate it and that's all.'

'Well actually,' continued Eppie as she floated merrily on her back, 'I hardly ever ate Mum's cooking. I often just flushed it down the toilet.

'Although once,' Eppie said as she floated about, 'I must admit I wore two of

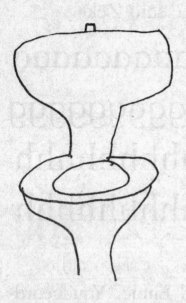

Mum's rissoles as shoes for a whole winter and another time I sent some of Mum's cookies to a war zone in Africa so the people could use them to build bomb shelters.'

'Eppie, could you perhaps fill us in on this later?' said Zeke as he doggy paddled furiously in a circle around Eppie. 'And in the meantime, could you try to remember that we're swimming in a saucepan of blood porridge?'

'Did you say blood porridge?' asked Eppie, horrified.

'Yes, I said blood porridge,' replied Zeke.

'Oh no, not blood porridge!'

'Oh yes yes, BLOOD PORRIDGE!!!!!!!!!'

'Oh,' whispered Eppie, 'I thought the voice said that he was Doug Dorridge.'

'Who, Madame Wormbutt, is Doug Dorridge?' yelled Zeke.

'I don't know,' said Eppie, 'but I thought he sounded cute.'

'I am cute,' said the saucepan of blood porridge, 'or at least I was very cute, before you two used your evil potions to turn me into this!'

'We didn't do anything,' said Eppie. 'We've only just arrived in this nightmare.'

'Don't you lie to me,' steamed the blood

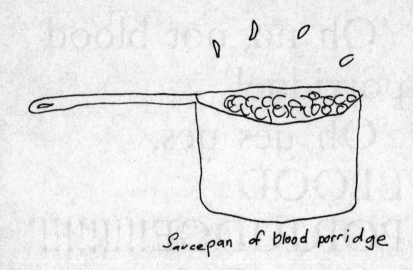

Saucepan of blood porridge

porridge. 'You two are Dr Freckle and Miss Hide 'n' Seek!'

'No we're not,' said Zeke and Eppie together.

'Of course you are. You look exactly like them,' blurted the blood porridge as he began to boil with rage. 'And it was you who turned me from a handsome hunk into this saucepan of yuk.'

('You were a handsome hunk?' giggled Eppie as she flirted and batted her eyelashes.

'Oh, don't be so desperate,' groaned Zeke.)

Now the bowl of blood porridge started to get really, really angry and his temper made his temperature rise . . . which made the blood porridge level rise . . . which meant that Zeke and Eppie, who were floating in the blood porridge were rising too . . . which meant that pretty soon Zeke and Eppie could quite possibly spill over the side of the saucepan . . . and land in the fire below.

'Have you anything to say before I boil you to blubber?' roared the blood porridge as he began to blup and then blurp and then bop blop ge plopfen.

'Well, yes . . . um . . . we . . . yes . . . um . . . we do,' said Zeke while he paddled furiously like a milkshake maker with his frantic little arms and legs.

'So hurry up and tell me what it is,' blabbed the blood porridge, 'or before you know it you'll both be caught in hot blood bubbles and spat into that bowl of eels' guts that are waiting to be eaten by bald vultures.'

bald vulture with one feather

'Well, Mr Blood Porridge,' said Zeke rather quickly as he boinged up and down in the bubbling blood. 'If we really were (boing) Dr Freckle and Miss Hide 'n' Seek (boing) and we really were able to change (boing) everything into

something (boing) different, don't you
think we would change you into a
fabulous blue swimming pool with a long
fun slippery dip (boing)?'

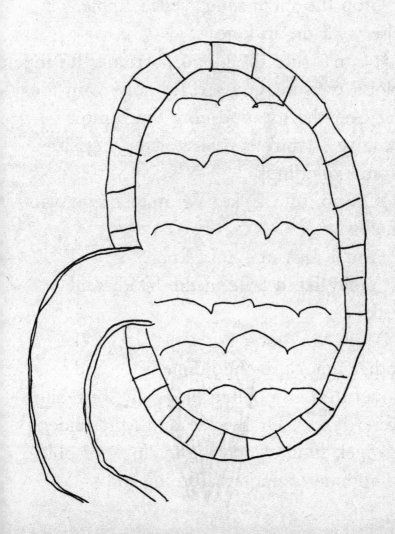

Well of course Zeke had a very good point and the saucepan of blood porridge realised this and became so excited that he started splattering all over the place.

'Stop the splattering,' yelled Eppie, 'or else we'll die in here.'

'I can't,' said the blood porridge. 'It's my blood pressure, you see. It's gone way too far over the top and now I'm almost positive I won't be able to stop myself from exploding!'

'Oh no,' said Zeke. 'We must prepare to die!'

'You'll miss me!' said Eppie.

'Yeah, like a hole in the head,' said Zeke.

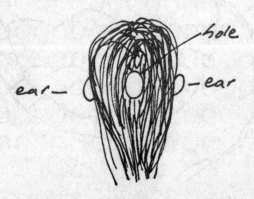

'I wish I had a head,' moaned the blood porridge. 'Even if it did have a hole in it.'

'Oh,' said Eppie, 'don't be upset. I think you look absolutely gorgeous just as you are.'

'You do?' said the blood porridge, suddenly becoming very calm and still.

'I do,' said Eppie with her fingers so tightly crossed that she nearly broke them off.

'Oh, that's so nice,' sighed the saucepan of blood porridge. 'Tell me, will you marry me?'

Well Eppie was just about to scream,

'Nooooooooooooooooooo
ooooooooooooooooooooo
ooooooooooooooooooooo
ooooooooooooooooooooo
ooooooooooooooooooooo
ooooooooooooooooooooo
ooooooooooooooooooooo

OOOOOOOO,' but before she could even open her mouth the saucepan of blood porridge tried to propose properly by bending down on his knees . . . and because he didn't have any knees, he tipped right off the edge of the stove and rolled all over the gooey black floor and drowned a dillion cocky cockroaches.

'H
e
l
p
!!!!!!' yelled Zeke as he was thrown out of the saucepan, hurtled through the air and landed kaplat on top of Eppie who was splat flat on the gooey black floor.

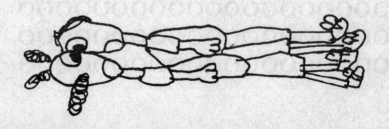

'Help,' squeaked Eppie as she lay squished under Zeke. 'GET OFF ME!'

But Zeke was actually extremely comfortable lying on Eppie and he was in no hurry to move.

'No, I won't get off you,' said Zeke calmly. 'I'm safe and dry and quite relaxed now and plan to stay here until help arrives.'

'You can't do that, what will Mum say?' said Eppie in the tiniest of squishy squishy voices.

'Well, considering that we're inside Mum's nightmare I guess that if she really likes you she won't say a thing and will just make something change in her thoughts so that we can get rescued quickly. And then I'll get off you. Now shut up because I want to have a snooze.'

'But . . .' said Eppie.

'But nothing,' said Zeke. 'Now be quiet and watch my eyebrows.' And with that

Zeke hypnotised Eppie by raising one eyebrow and then the other and then the other and then the other and then the other and then the other and then the other . . . left eyebrow up,

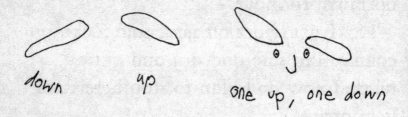

down   up   one up, one down

right eyebrow up, left eyebrow up, right up . . . really, really, really fast until Eppie fell deeply asleep. And once she was asleep Zeke was able to have the sort of little

nap that old people have when they're riding on buses. You know, when their mouths are wide open and flys fly in their gobs, do biz around their tonsils and then buzz out their ears.

'Snnnnnnnnnnnnnnnnnnnnnnnnnnnnnnnn nnnnnnore, huuuuuuuuuuuuuuuuugh, snoooooooooooooooooooooooore, huuuuu uuuuuuuuuumph, snorrrrrrrrrrrrrrrrrrrrrr rrrrrre, snoooooooooooooooooooooze,' snored Zeke so loudly that he didn't hear the clump clump clump of Dr Freckle and Miss Hide 'n' Seek's mutant mumbling servant (who answered to the name, Eeee-gord).

'Where is that blood porridge?' said Eeee-gord as he came trundling down the broken stone steps into the creepy kitchen. 'I must immediately get two bowls of blood porridge for the mad and evil Dr Freckle and Miss Hide 'n' Seek or they will turn me into something really horrible . . . like the piece of pickle on a flea-bitten hamburger.'

piece of pickle

Eeee-gord began to hear Zeke's sleeping snores as he approached the kitchen but he thought it was his rumbling stomach and told it to be quiet.

'I didn't say anything,' grumbled his stomach as it sat perched on Eeee-gord's shoulder.

'You're always telling me to stop doing this and stop doing that,' the stomach said acidly, 'and I find it very upsetting. You are so difficult to digest! You don't know what it's like to be a stomach stuck on a mumbling mutant moron's shoulder!

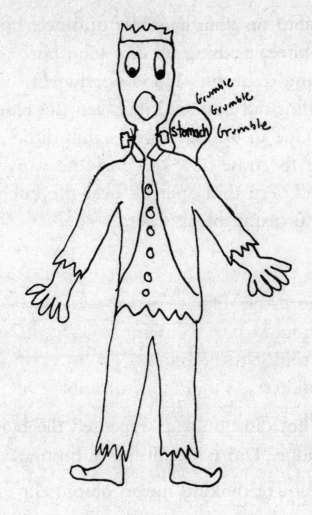

Honestly, all I really want to be is a famous opera singer in a long black dress with a bright orange wig because I hate spending my life sitting like Humpty

Dumpty on your shoulder and doing absolutely nothing all day long but chasing disgusting blood porridge!'

'What did you say?' bubbled the blood porridge in an extremely skinny little voice (because now of course he was spread very thin, spilt all over the kitchen's greasy grimy black floor).

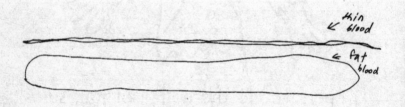

'What did you say?' repeated the blood porridge. 'Did you call me disgusting?

Oh, you're making me so absolutely furious that pretty soon I will lose control and become a tidal wave of blood porridge and you'll be swept through the window of a house where half a crocodile lives . . . and he will think you are his other half . . . and he'll glue you to his body and—'

'Oh shut up!' said the stomach and ate him.

And then the stomach started to perform a happy little dance on the mumbling mutant moron's shoulder.

'What are you doing!' bellowed Eeee-gord while Zeke and Eppie still miraculously managed to stay fast, snoozy, whoozy asleep.

'I'm performing the dance of joy,' said the stomach, 'because I have just eaten that annoying blood porridge.'

'You've what!' roared Eeee-gord. Well the stomach made himself as big as he could and then he told Eeee-gord that he'd eaten the blood porridge. And Eeee-gord got so incredibly angry that his face went purple and his

head blew off . . . and hit the ceiling . . .
and then landed THUMP on the floor.

But, surprisingly enough, his head could
still talk.

'You stupid stomach!' said Eeee-gord's
head. 'What are we going to feed Dr
Freckle and Miss Hide 'n' Seek? If we
don't give them the blood porridge they
asked for they'll be forced to suck our
blood and then they'll turn us into
something really dreadful.'

'What could be more dreadful than
this?' burped the stomach.

'Cow dung,' said Eeee-gord's head.

Eeee-gord and his stomach looked around the creepy kitchen for something to feed Dr Freckle and Miss Hide 'n' Seek. The room was gloomy dark but there was glowing green slime on the ceiling, millions of mice ran up the walls, massive cobwebs hung from the corners and something that looked a lot like puss was dripping out of the tap.

'Look!' said the stomach when he suddenly discovered the sleeping and sopping Zeke and Eppie. 'I can see a big double blob of porridge! So what I suggest is we suck it up somehow, saw it in half, put a bit in each bowl and then make the bowls look really full by filling them up to the very top with a mixture of tomato sauce and red cordial.'

'Good idea,' said Eee-gord politely. Then he took off his mouth and took off his ear and made them into a telephone

using a green rotting sausage from the
bottom of the fridge.

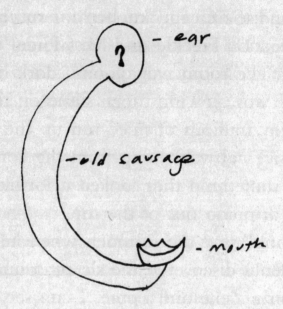

'Hello, is that emergency services?' Eeee-
gord said into the sausage. 'I desperately
need something here to suck up two blobs
and some rather thin blood.'

'Do you want a vampire?' asked the
operator.

'No, we need something that won't eat
the blood porridge and will be happy to
spit it out again.'

'Well, babies are good at spitting things out and we have seven baby leeches you could use and they're really very cheap.'

'No, you see we have no money.'

'Oh well, you need a real sucker then,' said the operator. 'What about a straw?'

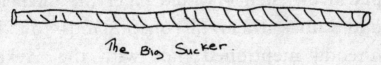

The Big Sucker.

As it turned out, the straw was busy sucking up to some old rich guy in a bar, so that left Eeee-gord and Stomach with only one solution.

• • • • • • • • • •

Meanwhile, Zeke and Eppie were still fast asleep,

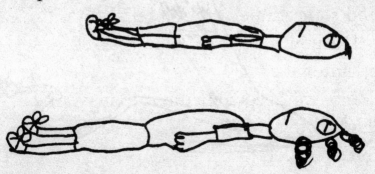

and had absolutely no idea what was about to happen. Sure, they could have guessed that Zeke might fart (sorry), fluff (sorry), bottom burp (hope that's not too rude), or that the spilt blood porridge might suddenly turn into Brad Pitt or that some humungous putrid evil stench would enter the kitchen and knock them all unconscious (oh, I already mentioned that with the 'Zeke bottom burp' thing). Well anyway, they simply never ever would have guessed that a wild vacuum cleaner would come careering into the kitchen – but then again, it was their mother's nightmare.

'I've come to suck ze blood!' roared the vacuum cleaner. And with that it sucked up Eppie and it sucked up Zeke and it tumbled down the scary stone steps (with Zeke and Eppie rattling inside it) to a damp dungeon way underground.

Headless Eeee-gord tried to follow the vacuum cleaner but as he ran he slipped on the slime and went sliding and ga-liding on his big fat bum all the way across the room, where his arms and legs fell off and his body promptly rolled and rolled and rolled and rolled until a fat cat with fourteen faces mistook him for a fish and ate all of him!

Then the cat vomited up the stomach and said, 'Whoah, I can't stomach that.'

'Free at last,' said the stomach as she bounced over to the fridge, stuck an orange on her head and began to sing her beloved opera.

But what about Zeke and Eppie? Well

deep inside the vacuum cleaner they were woken up by the terrifying sound of the stomach as she practised her opera singing.

'OOOOOOOOOOOOOOOOO OOOOOOOOOOOOOOOOOOO OOOOOOOOOooooooooooooooooo ooooooooooouuuuuuuuuuuuuuuuuu uuuuuuuuuuuuuuuuuuuuuuuuuuuuu ghaaaaaaaaaaaaaaaaaaaaaaaaaaaaa aaaaaaaaaaaaaaaaaaaaaaaaaaaaaaar.'

'Can you hear that?' said a very scared Eppie.

'Of course I can,' whimpered Zeke. 'And I'm pretty sure it's a ghost.'

'Nothing wrong with a ghost,' said the eavesdropping vacuum cleaner as they bounced from scary stone stair to scary stone stair. 'I myself was once a ghost and they were the happiest thousand years of my life.'

'So what happened?' asked Zeke and Eppie.

'Pardon?' said the vacuum cleaner, 'I can't hear you clearly from all the way inside me.'

'I said *So what happened?*' repeated Zeke.

'Pardon?' said the vacuum cleaner.

'He said, *So what happened?*' said Eppie.

'I'm sorry,' said the vacuum cleaner, 'but if you really want to make yourselves heard you are going to have to speak into my hose.'

'Did she say speak into her nose?' said Eppie.

'No!' yelped Zeke. 'She said speak into her toes!'

'But she doesn't have any toes!' said Eppie.

'Then she must have said to speak into her pantyhose!' said Zeke.

'**OH GROSS**,' said Eppie and Zeke together as they clutched their throats and rolled their eyes and fainted flat kaplat.

'Hey wake up!' said four sultanas, eight

balls of dust, two buttons and five hair bands. 'We'll tell you what happened.'

And so it came to be that everything that had been sucked up by the vacuum cleaner began to talk at once. There was quite a ruckus and it was impossible to understand a word until a dead slug yelled, 'LET ME SPEAK.' And so it did.

'Now what happened to me is the very same thing that happened to everyone here,' said the dead slug. 'Not long ago this land was a dreamland that existed in a mother's mind. Our land was ruled by a boy called Zeke and a girl called Eppie, who were the prince and princess of their mother's thoughts. But then one day the two children disappeared and no one knew where they went. Some say they went into outer space, some say they went under the sea, some say they got lost inside a storybook, and some say they were swallowed.'

'Gulp,' gulped Zeke quietly to Eppie, 'actually all those things happened to us.'

'But,' continued the dead slug, not hearing Zeke and Eppie's whisperings, 'wherever they went one thing is sure, and that is that their mother missed them dreadfully and her sweet thoughts turned bad and bleak as she became sadder and sadder. So, because of that the lovely Zeke and Eppie who once ruled this dreamland turned into the nightmare wicked characters of evil who are now known as Dr Freckle and Miss Hide 'n' Seek!'

'And they're the ones who have changed everything lovely here into something scary,' said a dust-covered drawing pin.

'And they're the ones who turned this dreamland into a nightmare world,' said the drawing pin's girlfriend who was a marble called Mable.

'Oh no,' said Eppie, as she quietly cried.

'This is all because Zeke got his yo-yo stuck in my hair and that's what started all our adventures far away from Mum.'

'No, it's not my fault, it's yours,' said Zeke. 'I mean it was your hair my yo-yo got stuck in.'

'Is not my fault,' said Eppie.

'Is so,' said Zeke.

'Is not,' said Eppie.

'Is so,' said Zeke.

'I—'

'See what I mean? It's a nightmare,' interrupted the vacuum cleaner. 'I used to be a heart-shaped flower.'

'Oh sob sob sob sob sob sob sob sob sob sob sob sob sob sob,' sobbed Eppie as her shoulders heaved like waves in the sea and her entire face looked like a big red round clown's nose.

And Zeke felt so incredibly sorry for his sister that he . . . (now don't tell anyone about this) . . . well . . . he put his arm around Eppie. But then he immediately got girl's germs and fell in love with the Back Street Boys and began giggling at absolutely nothing until he started crying, 'Oh boohoo boohoo.'

'Oh sob sob,' sobbed Eppie.

'Oh boohoo boohoo,' boohooed Zeke.

'Oh sob sob,' sobbed Eppie.

'Oh boohoo boohoo,' boohooed Zeke.

'Oh sob sob,' sobbed Eppie.

'Oh boohoo boohoo,' boohooed Zeke.

'Oh for heaven's sake you two,' said the vacuum cleaner. 'You're making such a fuss inside me that you're giving me the hiccups.' And with that the vacuum cleaner let out the most enormous belch and Zeke and Eppie came shooting out the hose and landed on a scorpion's tail on the slater-covered dungeon floor.

'Quick, jump!' yelled Zeke.

So Eppie jumped on Zeke, and Zeke jumped as far as he could with Eppie on his back and landed on . . . a hot iron.

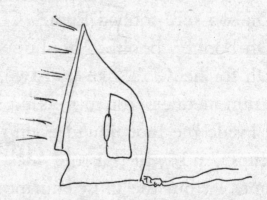

'Oh my cord!' said the iron as he sprayed shots of steam that just missed Zeke and Eppie. 'Its Dr Freckle and Miss Hide 'n' Seek! Quick, Mummy! Come and get them.'

Well, before you could say 'Rub your tummy mummy!', out of the darkest spookiest corner came an eerie figure dressed from head to toe in absolutely nothing except one very, very long bandage.

'Lucky they had such a long bandage and not just a packet of plasters,' whispered Eppie, 'or they would have had to place them very strategically.'

'Oh, be quiet Eppie!' said Zeke angrily. 'Can't you just concentrate on staying alive!'

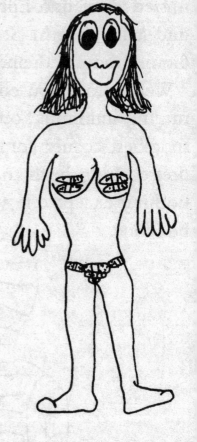

But what could they do as they sat perched on an iron . . . with the vacuum cleaner blocking the stairs, and its hose swinging wildly like a whip . . . and coming straight for them was the mummy with its arms outstretched, knocking over everything in its way.

'Get back,' yelled Eppie to the mummy, 'or we'll . . . um . . . or we'll . . . um . . . or we'll um . . . Zeke, what will we do?'

'We'll agh . . . We'll ur . . . We'll . . . call you rude names,' shouted Zeke, 'like, um, Dummy Mummy! And we'll, um, stick a note on your bottom that says Mum's Bum, and . . .

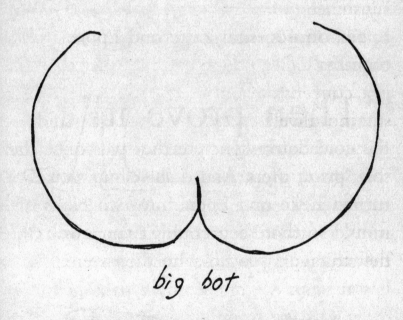

big bot

'Why don't you just turn me into a puddle?' teased the mummy.

'Because we're not Dr Freckle and Miss Hide 'n' Seek!' blustered Eppie.

'Are you sure?' said the stone stair that used to be a flowing stream.

'Are you positive?' said the creepy cobweb that used to be a golden pony.

'Do you cross your hearts and hope to die?' said the slimy wall that was once the sunshine.

'Yes, oh yes,' said Zeke and Eppie together.

'Then prove it!' said the cold damp concrete that was once the soft spring grass. And a snivelling snake turned Zeke and Eppie into two blobs of mould so that they couldn't run away before they'd proven who they were.

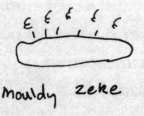

mouldy zeke

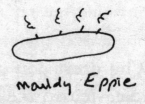

mouldy Eppie

'OK!' said mouldy Zeke, 'We'll prove we're not Dr Freckle and Miss Hide 'n' Seek.'

But how can you prove that you're not someone else? AND HOW DO YOU PROVE YOU'RE NOT EVIL? Well of course you could give a list of all the nice things that you've done in your life, or show photos of yourself being kind, or you could wait until someone else got into trouble and make a big point out of helping them. But how do you prove that you're sweet Zeke and Eppie when you look exactly like the two most evil creatures that have ruined the lives of all those around you?

Well, Eppie-the-blob-of-mould decided to prove that she and Zeke were really, really nice by explaining just what had happened to them. And she talked about getting caught in a nightmare and landing on a pirate ship and how she and

Zeke normally lived in a house on Earth and ate cereal for breakfast and Vegemite sandwiches for lunch and burnt chops and sausages for dinner and sometimes ice-cream for dessert. And she told the crowd how the two of them went to school with Miss Snailheadface and got chased by bullies and dobbed in by goody-two-shoes and how they had to do their homework and brush their teeth and wash behind their ears . . . and how they really, really wished that all they ever had to do was play computer games and eat rubbish!

'What!' said a jar of gollobuling black potion that used to be clear fresh air. 'You want to eat garbage from a bin! But the mere thought is evil!'

'No,' explained Eppie quickly, squishing up her nose. 'Rubbish is the word that describes anything that tastes nice. You can ask my mum if you don't believe me.'

And then the crowd clapped and

cheered and said they trusted Zeke and Eppie and a giant blowfly turned them back into their normal selves. And Eppie showed her gratitude by performing a brand new happy dance called *Oooh baby baby baby shake* 'em.

Now normally when anyone or anything sees Eppie dance they immediately collapse in a state of shock but, because this was Nightmare Land, all of the audience loved Eppie's dance and they all started jiving along and getting down and shakin' their booty. That is until Eppie called out, 'Hey, isn't this wicked!' and suddenly everyone stopped.

'Did she say wicked?' gasped the crowd.

'So she and her brother must be evil,' said a stinging jellyfish that was floating around in the dungeon. 'Quick someone arrest them!'

Then a big green ghoul covered in goop came trundling out of a greasy hole in the ground and using his spare old rattling chains promptly chained Eppie to Zeke.

'Oh gross,' moaned Zeke. 'Do I have to be chained to my sister? Couldn't I please be tied to that melting monster in the corner or at least to that enormous squirming tongue that is standing there all by itself?'

'No you can't,' said the mummy in a voice just like a mum. 'You'll do as you're told and be tied to your sister. And if you complain you won't be allowed to watch any television for at least five hundred years.'

'Have you got a television here?' Zeke asked excitedly.

'No,' said the mummy. 'I don't even know what one is. It just seemed like the sort of thing a mummy should say.'

And with that little Zeke and Eppie were placed in an enormous spoonful of the most disgusting cough medicine, and all the creatures that were part of the nightmare stood in a circle, stared at Zeke and Eppie and made scary squishy noises.

'I can't believe it,' said the black crow. 'I can't believe we've captured Dr Freckle and Miss Hide 'n' Seek.'

'I know,' meowed the cat that brings bad luck. 'I can't believe we've overcome their power.'

'Yes,' croaked the warty toad that was once a brilliant rainbow. 'It does seem rather extraordinary.'

'Yesssssssssssssssssssssssssssssssssssssssssssssss it doesssssssssssssssssssssssssssssssssssssss,' said the silent but deadly fart.

'In fact,' said the fanged man-eating

mosquito that buzzes round your head at night when you're trying to get to sleep, 'I find this situation so extraordinary that I suspect there is evil underfoot.'

And with that everyone immediately jumped up to look under their feet.

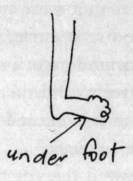

under foot

'Perhaps this is a joke,' howled the werewolf that was once a sunny beach. 'I mean, if these two really don't have the power to change us into things maybe they're not the wicked versions of themselves after all.'

'Indeed,' said the creaking door that used to be a double chocolate thick shake. 'There is only one way to tell if these creatures are tricking us, and that is to take them up to Skeleton Mountain. There the Head Ghost will use the full moon to take an x-ray of them and we'll be able to see straight through these two and discover what they're hiding.'

'Huuuuuuuuuuuuuuuuuuuuuuuuuuuuuuuuu uuuuuuuuuuuuuuuuuuuuuuuuuuuuuuuuuuuuu uuuuuuuuuuuuuugh,' said every single thing that was down in the dungeon that could make that *huuuuuuuuuuuuuuuuuuuuuuu uuuuuuuuuuuuuuuuuuuuuuuuuuuuuugh* sort of noise.

'But does that mean they'll see my Barbie doll underpants?' whimpered Zeke. 'I hope so,' giggled Eppie.

And so a long procession was formed as the sad nightmare ghouls and goblins and monsters and clanging chains and howling winds and sudden bumps and shivers-up-the-spine turned Zeke and Eppie into a pair of stinking old gym shoes and then followed the two of them as they trundled up to Skeleton Mountain.

oh pong!

old gym shoe

'Do you think we could call a cab?' said Eppie after a while as they turned right onto the river of earwax.

'No, I don't think they have cabs here,' said Zeke. 'I think they just have evil eels, planes that crash and insects that burrow under your skin and live there for ever and ever.'

So on they marched.

'You know what my worst nightmare is?' said Eppie.

'Let me guess,' said Zeke. 'That your hair isn't brushed?'

'No, my worst nightmare is that I get up and go to school one morning and forget to put my clothes on.'

'I can assure you,' said Zeke, 'that seeing you in the nude, is absolutely everyone's nightmare.'

On and on and on they walked, past their mother's most frightening nightmarish thoughts. Here they saw a train that had caught on fire, there they saw a grocery bill of eight million dollars, far away they saw Neville The Nerd from the newsagency asking Mum on a date, and over there they saw their mum walking to the corner shop with the back of her dress accidentally tucked into her knickers. Oooops!

But still they wandered on. And now, through the holes where their shoelaces were threaded, Zeke and Eppie could see their mother's frightening fears about what had happened to her darling children. In one they saw their mother crying as she searched the streets in vain, in another they saw their mother frantically banging on a hospital's closed door, and in another they saw their mum scooping up mush and saying very bossily, 'I told you that if you drank too much fizzy drink your insides would explode!'

But still the weary Zeke and Eppie and their kooky, spooky companions wandered on and on and on . . . past empty milk cartons that had been put back in the fridge, public telephones that were always broken, and old ladies who bashed supermarket trolleys into the back of your ankles . . . until finally the procession arrived at the base of Skeleton Mountain.

'Oh thank heavens there's an elevator!' said Eppie happily as she looked up the mountain with her shoe tongue hanging out.

'The elevator's broken,' said Zeke sadly.

'Arrrrrrrrrrr, what a nightmare!' wailed Eppie.

And so the procession began to climb the mountain. Through the forest of the dead they wandered, past bulging eyes that had no bodies and past frightening rustles of leaves. Zeke and Eppie thought they saw things that didn't exist and they felt things that they couldn't see, and . . . they smelt things that were themselves . . . stinky old gym shoes.

The wind was cold, so bitterly cold and for every step they took forward they seemed to move more than two steps back.

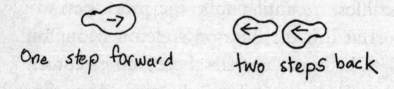

One step forward

two steps back

Finally Zeke and Eppie could go no further and stopped by their mother's second worst nightmare . . . a set of bathroom scales.

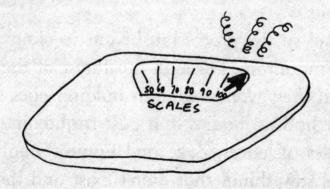

SCALES

'Tell the spooky people we have to stop,' said Eppie to a scab that would never heal.

'They have to stop!' the scab told the biting wind who then carried the message up the mountain until it got tangled in a death valley and echoed and echoed in a most annoying way way way way way.

But at least the message was heard by the head of the ghosts – or the Headless Head of the Ghosts, as he was more accurately called.

the head
was here

The headless Head Ghost

'What do you mean, they're too tired to come up?' said the headless Head Ghost. 'What sort of baddies are they? Surely if they really were Dr Freckle and Miss Hide 'n' Seek they'd put on a better show of bravery than this!'

'It may be a trick,' said the bossy teacher's pet who, let's face it, is everyone's nightmare. 'I suspect the prisoners may be very evil and are desperately trying to cover it up.'

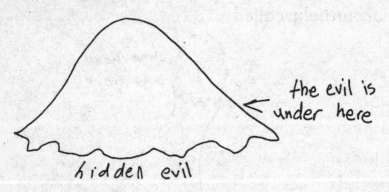

the evil is under here

hidden evil

'Then I have no choice but to zoosh-fly-swoop down to them,' said the headless Head Ghost 'and see if I can see through their trickery.'

'Oh bravo,' said the bossy teacher's pet, because she was also a crawler.

Well the headless Head Ghost wanted to zoosh-fly-swoop but honestly by the time he'd ironed his official Head Ghost sheet and fastened all his medals he was running far, far, far too late to zoosh-fly-swoop. So he grabbed Skeleton Mountain's polaroid camera, hopped on the sort of rain cloud that ruins every picnic, and poured down on the bottom of the mountain instead. Splatter splatter splatter splatter splatter. And then the ghost pulled himself together, dried himself off with a portable ghost dryer and summoned the very tired Zeke and Eppie-stinky-gym-shoes.

Ghostdryer

'First I must change them back to what they were,' said the headless Head Ghost, loudly. And with that he clicked his fingers and Zeke and Eppie turned into tiny crying babies. Well, sure enough, they were babies once, but I think the ghost probably meant to turn them into something a little more recent.

'Here, let me try,' said the disease that had freshly escaped from a bottle in Horror Hospital. So sure enough the disease tried to change Eppie and Zeke into what they were before and as a result Eppie and Zeke turned into yo-yos and sea slugs and aliens and full stops and finally they changed into themselves.

'Ah,' said the headless Head Ghost with relief, 'I guess now we can begin.'

Of course there was a rattle and squeak and bang and creak and groan while the spooky creatures gathered to watch the headless Head Ghost as he took a see-through photo of Zeke and Eppie and waited for it to develop.

And when it developed the nightmare creatures watched the headless Head Ghost take a deep breath and stare first at the photo of Zeke and then at the photo of Eppie and then at the one of Zeke and then at the one of Eppie again. And then they saw him do it again and sort of start to giggle. Then the headless Head Ghost did it again and again and again and then he quietly started to guffaw.

'Well,' said the impatient vampire, who was running late for his supper and had a low blood sugar level which was making him very grumpy, 'can you see goodness or evil inside them?'

'Yes,' clanged the crowd, 'are they Dr Freckle and Miss Hide 'n' Seek?'

'I ha ha ha don't know,' tittle-giggled the headless Head Ghost.

'What!' squawked the vultures.

'I don't know,' laughed the Head of the Ghosts, 'because I just can't concentrate!'

'But why?' chorused the crowd, who were all spitting and sweating and growing agitated.

'Because the . . . because the . . . because the . . .' mumbled the headless Head Ghost.

'Yes!' squawked the vulture.

'Because,' said the headless Head Ghost, trying as hard as he could to stop laughing, 'the male creature appears to be a ha ha ha ha ha ha ha . . . wearing Barbie doll underpants! And the small female, who I think is only about eight years old, appears to be ha ha ha ha ha . . . wearing . . . a . . . ha ha ha . . . bra.'

'What!' giggled the crowd.

'What the heck are you wearing a bra for?' whispered Zeke.

'I'm not wearing a bra,' said Eppie

loudly. 'It's just that when we fell out of the blood porridge and plummeted down through the air, all that gravity gave me a wedgie which I simply haven't had time to fix up.'

'But a wedgie doesn't look like a bra!' said Zeke.

'It does if it's a really, really high wedgie,' said Eppie.

'Well, that was a complete failure,' said the fog as it wandered

really, really high wedgie

across the ground. 'I've never known a head ghost not to see through people and find if they are good or evil. So now what can we do?'

'I suggest,' said a boring queue that just grew longer and longer. 'I suggest that we have no alternative but to call Frankenslime. And we shall have him remove the so-called "Zeke and Eppie's" hearts and test them for sincerity.'

'Huuuuuuuuuuuuuuuuuuuuuuuuuuuuuuuuu uuuuuuuuuuuuuuuuuuuuuuuuuuuuuuuuuuuuu uuuuuuuuuuuuuuuugh,' said every single thing that was at the base of Skeleton Mountain and could make that *Huuuuuuu uuuuuuuuuuuuuuuuuuuuuuuuuuuuuuuuuuuuuuu uuuuuuuuuuuuuuuuuuuuuuuuuuuuuuuuuuuugh* sort of noise.

'Frankenslime,' whispered Eppie to Zeke. 'Oh, he sounds powerful and exciting and just like Leonardo di Caprio. I bet he's really gorgeous.'

Leonardo di Caprio

Suddenly there was a tremendous kerblobblebubble slurp and an enormous dribble of slime came slooping toward Zeke and Eppie from just behind the mountain.

'Huuuuuuuuuuuuuuuuuuuuuuuuuuuuuuuuuuuu uuuuuuuuuuuuuuuuuuuuuuuuuuuuuuuuuuuuu uuuuuuuuugh,' said every single thing that suddenly saw Frankenslime and could make that *Huuuuuuuuuuuuuuuuuuuuuuu uuuuuuuuuuuuuuuuuuuuuuuuuuuuuuuuuuugh* sort of noise.

'Oh shut up,' slop-snorted Frankenslime as he came to a sudden stop right in the middle of the crowd.

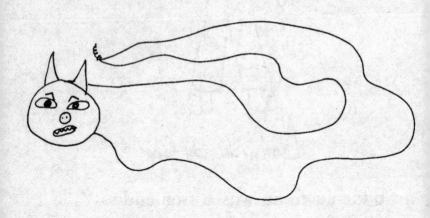

'So do you still think he's cute?' said Zeke in disgust.

'Cuter than you,' said Eppie quickly. 'But then so is a baboon's butt, so I guess that doesn't mean much.'

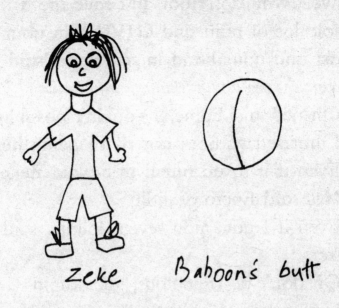

zeke   Baboon's butt

'Anyway,' whispered Eppie, 'when you and I become the prince and princess of this land and everything gets turned back to the wonderful thing that it was, then I reckon this ugly slime will become the most handsome of handsome Prince Charmings, because the more horrible something seems in this nightmare the more wonderful it will be back in Dreamland.'

'Well, why don't you just save me a whole lot of pain and give him your heart and your hand in marriage,' said Zeke.

'Oh no,' said Eppie, 'I couldn't possibly get married without our mum being here.'

'Even if it saved our lives?' asked Zeke.

'No,' said Eppie grandly.

'Even if I gave you seven dollars,' said Zeke.

'Oh don't be ridiculous, you stupid sheepdog brains,' said Eppie.

'All right, what about seven-fifty,' said Zeke.

'Deal,' said Eppie with a grin.

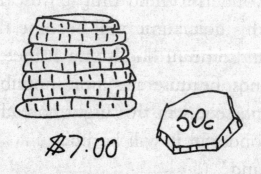

But all this time the dreaded Frankenslime was excitedly sharpening his heart-cutting knives. And when he'd finished he licked his super slimy lips, spat on Zeke and Eppie's faces and said, 'Is there anything you'd like to say before I remove your hearts?'

'Ah, yes,' said Zeke, 'Your breath smells disgusting!'

'KILL HIM,' said Frankenslime. 'Remove his innards and feed them to the budgerigars who sing Spice Girl medleys.'

'NO WAIT!!!!!!!!!'

thundered Eppie. 'I have something to say . . . I would like to save my brother's life and marry Frankenslime.'

'Huuuuuuuuuuuuuuuuuuuuuuuuuuuuuuuu uuuuuuuuuuuuuuuuuuuuuuuuuuuuuuuuuuu uuuuuuuuugh,' said every single thing that couldn't believe Eppie wanted to save her brother's life, (and could make that

Huuuuuuuuuuuuuuuuuuuuuuuuuuuugh sort of noise).

'Oh be quiet!' said Zeke. 'I'm paying her $7.50.'

'Are you quite sure you want to marry Frankenslime?' said a sort of crack in the footpath that you always trip over. 'I mean, are you quite sure you want to marry this grot?'

'Yes,' said Eppie. 'I've lived with a grotty brother all of my life, so being married to a grot can't be much different.'

'Gee, thanks a lot,' mumbled Zeke.

'Then you are without doubt Eppie the Princess and Zeke the Prince,' said a freezing cold shower, 'for only those with goodness in their hearts could see any beauty in scum like Frankenslime.'

'Hoooooray!' cried all the spooky creatures. 'At last our Prince and Princess are back!'

'Quick, let them marry,' said the sort of pong that lingers. 'Let her marry the slime and prove she's not tricking us.'

'Yes, let the festivities begin!' howled all the hyenas and jackals together, sounding like a car alarm.

And so the celebrations commenced at the nearest haunted castle, and what a nightmare the celebrations were. First

Eppie couldn't fit into her dress, and then the colour didn't suit her. Then there was a traffic jam on the way to the party and when Eppie arrived she quickly discovered that her frock was the same as the one four werewolves were wearing. Then the cake was stale and the lemonade was flat and it started to rain and Eppie's hair went all fuzzy and the slime ate too much and leant over the balcony and was sick all over his slime-sister.

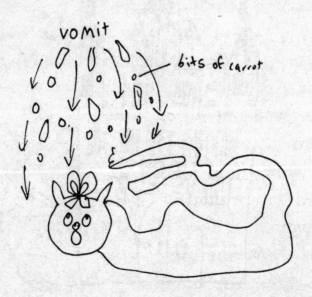

vomit

bits of carrot

'Oh isn't this great,' said Eppie as she stood in the weeds that grew in the church entrance and prepared for Zeke to 'give her away'. 'Soon Mum will be happy again and she'll concentrate really hard and help us leave this land of bad thoughts and we'll return home safely.'

'Yeah,' said Zeke. 'I'm so excited!'

'I'm more excited,' said Eppie.

'No! I'm more excited,' said Zeke.

'Let the ceremonies begin,' chanted the crowd impatiently.

'No,' said Frankenslime. 'We must wait for my sister to change out of her frock because it's covered in vomit.'

'Oh, isn't that sweet!' said the crowd and then they waited and waited and waited and waited.

And then, when his slime-sister reappeared,

dressed in a very lovely purple polka dot dress with four matching polka dot shoes, Frankenslime smiled a weird little smile, snort-sla-slurped a massive sigh of relief and said the ceremony could begin.

So the band started playing, completely out of tune and out of time and Eppie tripped on her own dress, and Frankenslime slopped all over the guests, and the priest started to laugh and everyone started to mutter and the whole thing went absolutely perfectly . . . for a nightmare, that is.

And when they got to the spot where they were to say their vows, Frankenslime took Eppie's hand in his filthy floppy fingers and she looked into his little grubby eyes and imagined the handsome prince that he would become as soon as she kissed his lips. But Zeke saw Frankenslime wink at his Franken sister and suddenly Zeke became deeply suspicious.

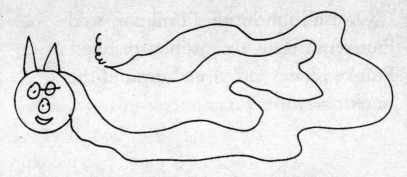

Then the priest began the wedding service and asked if anyone in the audience had any reason why this slime and this princess should not be wed and Zeke suddenly yelled, 'I do!'

'You do what?' said the priest.

'I do have a reason why they should not be wed,' said Zeke.

'Oh be quiet,' said Eppie as she puckered up to kiss the slime.

'Yes be quiet!' said Frankenslime's sister.

'I know,' interrupted Frankenslime, 'why don't we all have a quick relaxing drink before the ceremony finishes and that will calm us all down and we'll become friends.'

'Oh isn't my brother brilliant,' said Frankensister as she grubby-grinned at Frankenslime and passed around the smoking swine wine.

A glass of swine Wine

'No wait!' cried Zeke as all the creepy creatures grabbed the swine wine and raised their glasses to their lips. 'Do not let a drop touch your tongues because this filthy slime is Dr Freckle in disguise!'

'Huuuuuuuuuuuuuuuuuuuuuuuuuuuuuuuuuu uuuuuuuuuuuuuuuuuuuuuuuuuuuuuuuuuuuuuuuu uuuuuuuuuuuuuuuuugh,' said every single thing that was holding a wine glass and could make that *Huuuuuuuuuuuuuuuuuuuuu uuuuuuuuuuuuuuuuuuuuuuuuuuuuuuuuuuuuuuuuuuuu uuuuuuuuuuuuuuuuuuuuuuuuuuuuuuuuuuuuuuuuuuuu uuuuugh sort of noise.*

'But how do you know that he's Dr Freckle?' said the bird poo that suddenly landed on Zeke's shoulder.

'Because Frankenslime is being nice to his sister, winking at her, waiting for her to change out of her vomit-covered dress . . . and doesn't anyone else wonder why!' said Zeke. 'Face up to it! The only time a brother is ever nice to his sister is when they've planned something nasty together.'

'Be quiet!' said Frankenslime.

'No, actually, surprisingly enough, Zeke is telling the truth,' said little Eppie. 'Because the only times Zeke is ever nice to me is when he needs me to help him with a dastardly plan, like hiding Leona Bluntbum's bicycle up a tree or colouring Willy Littlewilly's hair bright pink while he's asleep.'

Zeke and Eppie were right about the evil Frankenslime – sorry, I mean Dr Freckle – and his sister, Frankensister – sorry, I mean Miss Hide 'n' Seek – but sadly Zeke and Eppie were too late because all around the ghostly ballroom the greedy, creepy creatures had already sipped their smoking swine wine and were turning into the most horrifying

nightmarish thing in the world . . . poo
on the bottom of a shoe.

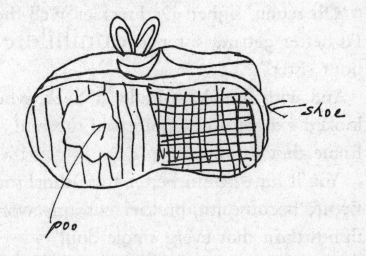

'Stop!' yelled Zeke.

But there was nothing they could do.

And that's when Dr Freckle who looked
like a slime turned into Dr Freckle who
looked like Zeke.

'So it's just you and me,' said Dr
Freckle.

'Not necessarily,' said Zeke. 'You see, I
have my super sister here and she will
fight with me against all evil until we
save the world!'

'What!' said Eppie.

'Be quiet!' said Zeke.

'Oh really,' sighed Dr Freckle. 'Well then I'd better get my sister to annihilate your sister!'

And with that Miss Hide 'n' Seek, who looked exactly like Eppie, told the real Eppie that she smelt.

'You'll have to do better than that,' said Eppie, 'because my brother calls me worse things than that every single day!'

'All right,' said Miss Hide 'n' Seek as she took an enormous breath. 'You look like an anaconda's appendix!'

'Oh, that's pathetic,' said dear sweet little Eppie. 'You'll have to do better than that!'

'You walk like a bandicoot,' added Dr Freckle.

'Your head looks like a g-string,' said Miss Hide 'n' Seek.

And so began a war of words, with Dr Freckle and Miss Hide 'n' Seek saying really horrible things to Zeke and Eppie. But none of them hurt until Dr Freckle said, 'And finally, your mother is a lemon head with a body like a potato . . . and she **never ever** loved you!'

Now there are some things you could say about Zeke and Eppie's mum – I mean sure she can't cook, and her favourite singer is Mariah Carey (oh gross!) and she dances like an overhead fan and she often gives incredibly boring speeches about being nice and being kind and eating all your dinner – but no matter what hideous, vile and revolting things she is guilty of, their mum has always, always, always, always, always loved Eppie and Zeke.

And Eppie and Zeke knew this and thought of their mum and were filled with love for her. And their mum felt their love and her own love rushed from her heart, into her veins, all the way through her body (which was a little chubbier now than before she had kids) and the love rushed up to her brain and into her thoughts and straight into her nightmare where her love found Eppie and Zeke and turned them into

superheros!!!!!!!

And before you could say biff

bang

wham

and fididdle de dee do wop wop widdle,

Dr Freckle and Miss Hide 'n' Seek had been tied in a knot and thrown down a

volcano where their odours of evil combined with a whole lot of gases and caused a massive volcanic eruption.

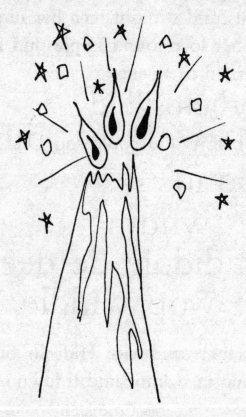

But the lava that flowed wasn't boiling red or even burning hot. Instead, it was a lava of brilliant gold that rolled down the mountain and turned the craggy bare rocks to soft green grass and the bare grey trees grew leaves and the cold chasms turned to bouncing fresh rivers and the birds . . . well, the birds . . . OK, the birds just stayed as birds, but nicer, chirpier, more delightful ones.

nicer, chirpier, more delightful birds

And the lava flowed down the mountain and over the haunted castle and turned it into a palace, and the sun began to shine, and the ghosts became princes and princesses, and the vultures became extraordinary musicians and the gardens were filled with people playing and laughing and giggling and everywhere there was happiness . . . Well, everywhere except for two important places – Zeke and Eppie's hearts.

'I want to go home,' said Zeke to Eppie.
'Me too,' said Eppie to Zeke.
'Well,' said Zeke. 'We'll have to make our mum think about us coming home so her thoughts can bring us back to her.'
So Zeke and Eppie thought about coming home, about running in the garden, and snuggling in their beds, and throwing Mum's burnt cooking out the window when she wasn't looking, and fighting over what to watch on television and about all three of them cuddling and pinching and laughing and laughing . . . and slowly Zeke and Eppie began to rise from the ground and they floated upwards

to the glorious sunshine where a gentle breeze blew them into the light and carried them whirling and swirling and gad–er–a–ling all the way through the blue sky and then slippery sliding down a brightly coloured rainbow.

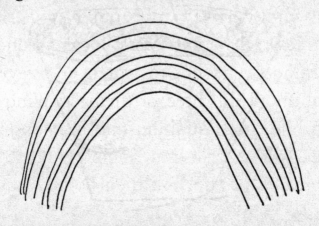

And when they reached the end of the rainbow they found a pot of treasure. And who should be sitting in it but their mum!

So Zeke and Eppie immediately surfed her thought waves and were heading straight back home, where they could become normal size again and live happily ever after.

* * * * * * * * *

Or at least that's what was meant to happen.

Except

that while Zeke and Eppie's mum was thinking about Zeke and Eppie she was holding their photos and walking to their bedrooms and when she got to Eppie's room she stood in the middle, and smiled at the walls that the three of them had painted together, and she laughed at the clothes in Eppie's wardrobe that were handed down from Zeke, and she wished and she wished that Zeke and Eppie were right there in her arms . . .

and

whoosh,

zooosh,

Zeke and Eppie were almost in her arms,

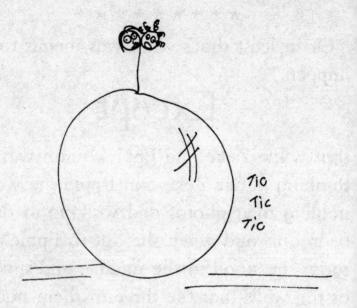

Tic
Tic
Tic

until Mum got distracted as she looked at the messy floor and thought 'Oh this room looks like a bomb's hit it.'

And that's where Zeke and Eppie ended up . . .

inside a bomb!

TO BE CONTINUED

About the author, Gretel Killeen:

Gretel Killeen started writing comedy by accident when she stood up to perform a very serious poem and everybody laughed.

From here she moved to writing and performing comedy in a variety of theatres and clubs across her home country, Australia, and for a number of major radio stations. Gretel's comedy writing then led to television and in 2001 Gretel hosted Australia's *Big Brother* – a phenomenal success which she repeated in 2002, 2003 and 2004.

Gretel has published a number of best-selling books that will split your sides and make your head explode. After you read them, you'll never be the same again.

She lives in Sydney's famous Bondi with her two children, Zeke and Eppie – the stars of *My Sister's a Yo-yo*, *My Sister's an Alien*, *My Sister's a Burp*, *My Sister's a Sea Slug* and *My Sister's a Full Stop*.

About the illustrators:

Zeke

Zeke was born in 1988 and is a fun-loving, phone-hogging Sagittarian. He likes surfing, cricket, football, chocolate drinks and teasing his little sister. When he grows up he wants to be incredibly rich so that he can live in a mansion and hire slaves to do all the work his mum does for him now.

Eppie

Eppie was born in 1991 and looked like a very pretty worm. She loves dancing, singing, composing songs and screaming loudly whenever her brother comes near. When she grows up she wants to be a banker, singer, actor, writer and teacher. And she also wants to marry a prince.

GRETEL KILLEEN

My Sister's a YO-YO

When Eppie falls into a pothole, gets **squashed** to the size of a **strawberry** and becomes completely **entangled** in her brother Zeke's **yo-yo**, Zeke only has a day to get her back to normal. What follows is a **hilarious** high tale of **escape**, theft, bullies, **brats**, goody-goodies, garbage trucks, **magic** lamps, **scabs**, snot, bribery, **bravery**, a blind mum, a fat nurse, a **skinny teacher** and a boy on a bicycle covered in something **very unsavoury** – and that's only the beginning!

'Short-every-second inventive fun'
JACQUELINE WILSON

0099433680

My Sister's an **Alien**

When Eppie gets **squished** to the size of a strawberry, ends up **flying** round the world, landing on planet sock and about to be kidnapped by a **handsome alien** prince, it's up to her brother Zeke to rescue her. What follows is a **laugh-a-minute** adventure full of short-sighted cats, space rockets, **burps**, possums, owls, **goodies**, **baddies**, galactic battles, **movie stars**, superstars, false **moustaches**, girls' nighties, flying horses, footballs, diamonds, **lovesick Martians** and motorbike rides with the man in the moon – and that's all before mum wakes up.

'Madly inventive and very funny'
JACQUELINE WILSON

0099433672

My Sister's a Sea Slug

When Eppie and Zeke get **stretched** like spaghetti it's only a matter of time before they are **sucked** down the plughole and into a new adventure. What follows is a **giggle-filled** non-stop underwater **romp**, with man-eating seaweed, pirates in petticoats, secret castles, **magic mermaids**, fat fisherman, **splendid** speedy sea cycles, **elastic** eels, and **supersonic** horses . . . and that's all before breakfast!

0099448076

GRETEL KILLEEN

My Sister's a

Burp

When the teeny-weeny Zeke and Eppie are accidentally swallowed by their mum they need to find a way to safety but first they need to wake up Mum's brain. What follows is a chock-a-block adventure full of jealous germs, evil eyes, bouncing bottoms, hysterical hair, ticklish teeth, arm armies and tap-dancing toes ... and that's all before Mum realises that Zeke and Eppie are even missing.

'Short-every-second inventive fun'
JACQUELINE WILSON

0099448084

gretEl KiLLeen

my Sister's a Full Stop

When tiny Eppie and tiny Zeke come shooting out of their mother's nose, they land slap-bang in the middle of a book of fairytales.

What follows is a madcap caper, full of laughing crocs, wicked warty witches and golden geese galore!
You'll love Zeke and Eppie's hilariously wacky adventures as they fight and fumble to escape the clutches of the ZANY fairytale world and find their way back home (but not back up Mum's nose!).

009946408X